THE ISLE OF DWARVES

WRITTEN & ILLUSTRATED BY

Massimiliano FREZZATO

ADAPTATION
BHARUCHA

HEAVY METAL

GRAPHICS: TESHI BHARUCHA

ONCE UPON A TIME THERE WAS THE TOWER... IT WAS EIZ 17, ON KOLONY, THE ICE CAP THAT COVERED THE PLANET HAD FINALLY MELTED, AND THE COLONISTS' CIVILIZATION WAS AT THE SUMMIT OF ITS SCIENTIFIC AND CULTURAL DEVELOPMENT... THIS PERIOD BECAME KNOWN AS THE AGE OF "GREAT SPLENDOR." NO ONE DREAMED THAT A CATACLYSM WAS ABOUT TO STRIKE... THEN, IN EIZ 18, THE DWARVES, AN OPPRESSED PEOPLE, REVOLTED AGAINST THEIR POSITION AT THE BOTTOM RUNG OF SOCIETY AND TRIED TO OVERTHROW THE HUMAN INHABITANTS OF THE TOWER... A BLOODY CIVIL WAR WAS WAGED FOR EIGHT EIZ, DURING WHICH ALL CONTACT WAS LOST BETWEEN THE TOWER AND THE COMMUNITIES OF SAGES WHO HAD SETTLED NEAR THE ISLANDS. SIXTY EIZ HAVE SINCE GONE BY. WITH THE PASSAGE OF TIME AND THE DEATHS OF THE EARLY SETTLERS, KNOWLEDGE AND TECHNICAL EXPERTISE HAVE BOTH BEEN WIPED OUT. FOR THE FEW SCATTERED GROUPS OF SURVIVORS, THE TOWER IS NO MORE THAN A LEGEND IN THE MISTS OF TIME. AND THEY ARE ALL FIRMLY CONVINCED THAT THEY ARE THE SOLE SURVIVORS OF A PLANET WHOSE NAME NO ONE REMEMBERS. IN SPITE OF HIMSELF, FANGO IS DRAGGED INTO A SERIES OF MISADVENTURES BY THE OLD TRAPPER ZERIT, WHOSE SOLE PURPOSE IN LIFE SEEMS TO BE TO FIND THE TOWER OF THE MASER. THEY END UP MAROONED ON A SMALL ISLE IN THE MIDDLE OF THICK FOG. BUT ALL IS NOT LOST... ERHA IS ALREADY OUT LOOKING FOR ZERIT...

1.

2.

4.

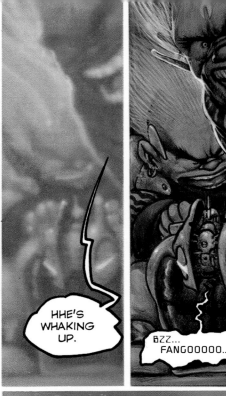

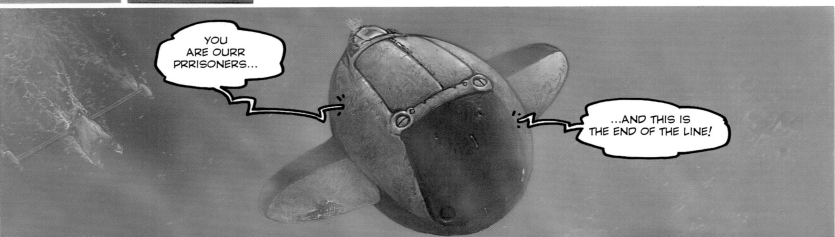

7.

* 1 LENGTH = APPROX. 3 YARDS

I JUST DON'T KNOW WHAT TO DO...

BEEP...

LISTEN, OLD FRIEND... WE HAVE TO FIND A WAY OF GETTING OUT OF HERE!

EASY TO SAY!

BOOOOM!

?

WHAWUZDAT? WHAT'S GOING ON HERE?

BEEP...

SO?

WAIT! I'M LOOKING FOR SIGNS OF THE EXPLOSION.

HNFF HHNNFF HNF

I CAN GET A VIEW OF THE WHOLE ISLAND FROM UP HERE.

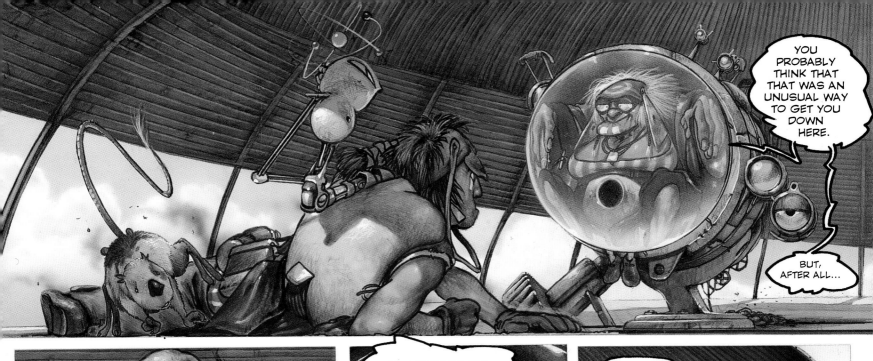

19.

21.

STUMPH

SQUNCH!

AHHH! SHOO! *GET OUT! SCRAM!* GET HIM AWAY FROM ME!

OOO! I'M ALLERGIC TO RATS... *ATCHOOOOOMM!*

GET HER!

HE'S GOT A LOT OF BALLS, THE LITTLE BRAT!

PLEEEEASE! HE'S *YOUR* RAT!

HE'S *NOT* MY RAT.

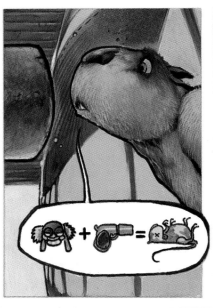

OH NO.... *ATCHOOOMM!*

HE IS *YOUR* RAT!

FROM NOW ON, HE BELONGS TO *YOU!*

HE HAS BEEN *IMPRINTED! ATCHOOOOOOOMM!*

22•

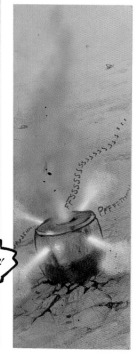

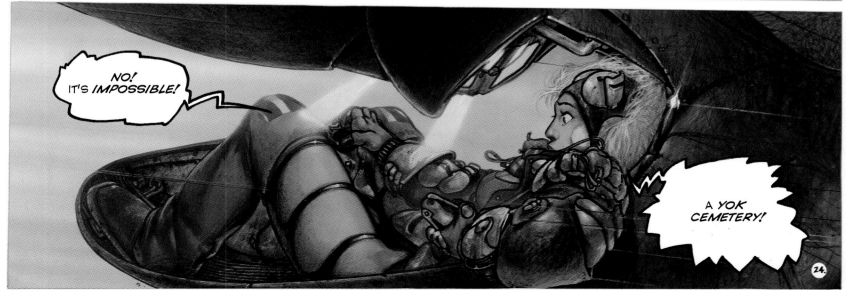

25.

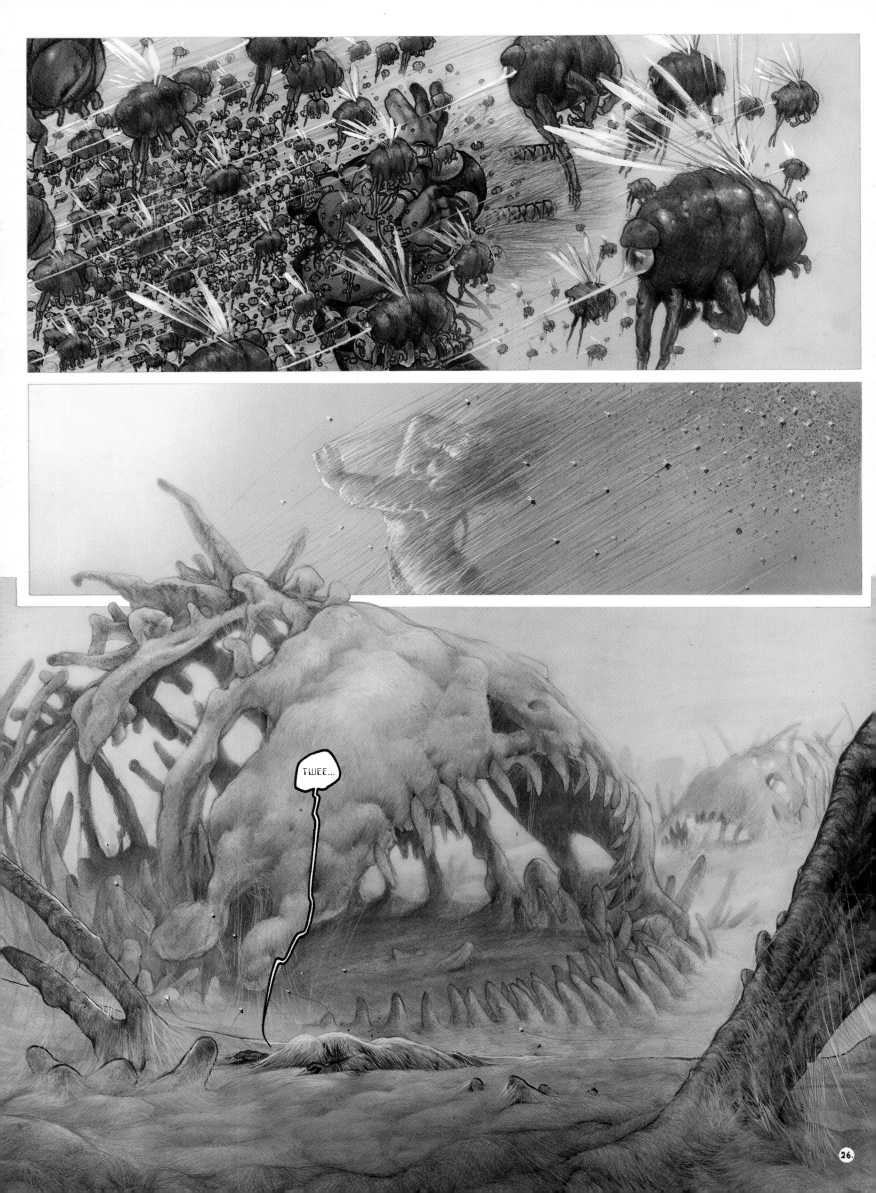

28

*ZOTH = ADJECTIVE IN DWARF LANGUAGE: RARE, VITAL, NECESSARY, INDISPENSABLE.

30.

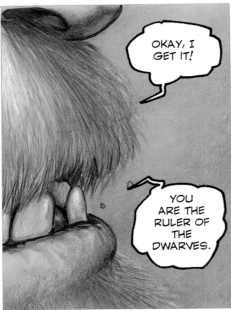

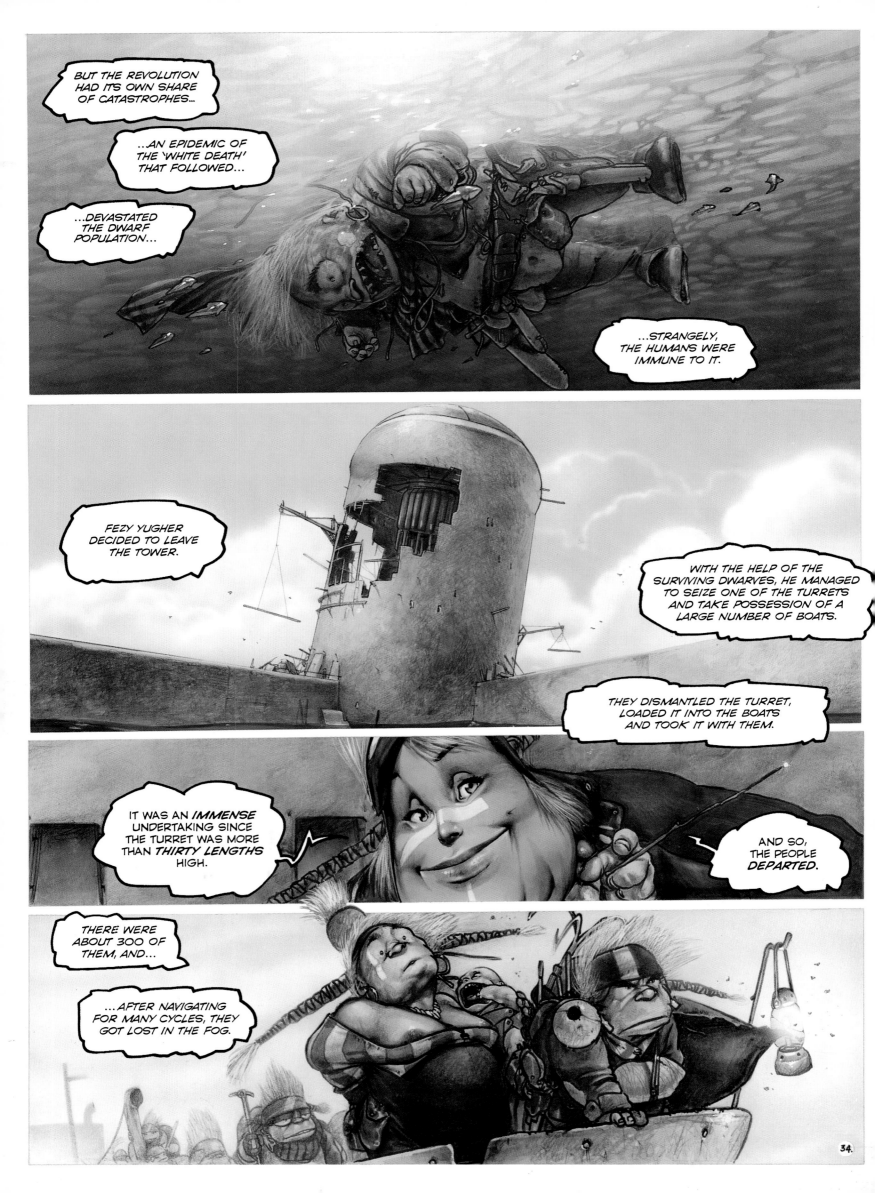

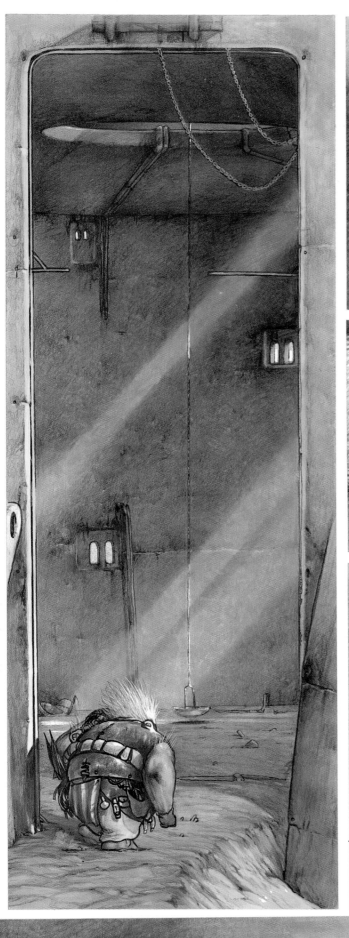

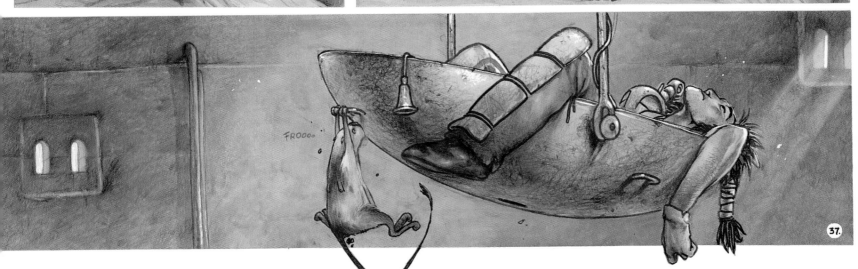

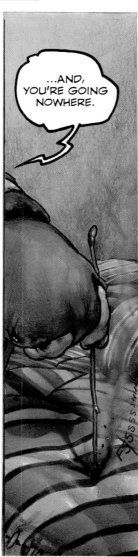

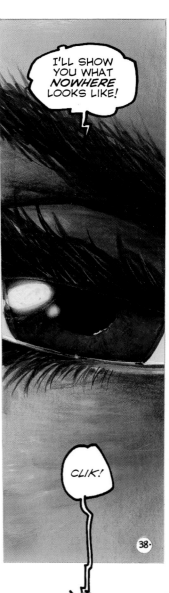

38

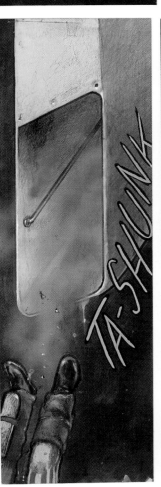

PLOP!

?!

...

ERHA!!!

SO...? YOU KNOW HER TOO?

WHAT HAVE YOU DONE TO HER?!

MY DWARVES *RESCUED* HER FROM THE SPIDER-FLIES.

...OF COURSE, SHE WAS ALSO *DISINFECTED*...

...WE CAN'T RISK THE POSSIBILITY OF CONTAGION FROM THE *WHITE DEATH*...

BUT DON'T WORRY... SHE'LL COME OUT OF IT VERY SOON...

YOUR FRIEND'S CONDITION IS MUCH *WORSE*. HE'LL NEED ALL THE HELP WE CAN GIVE HIM...

...BUT ENOUGH KIDDING AROUND...

41.

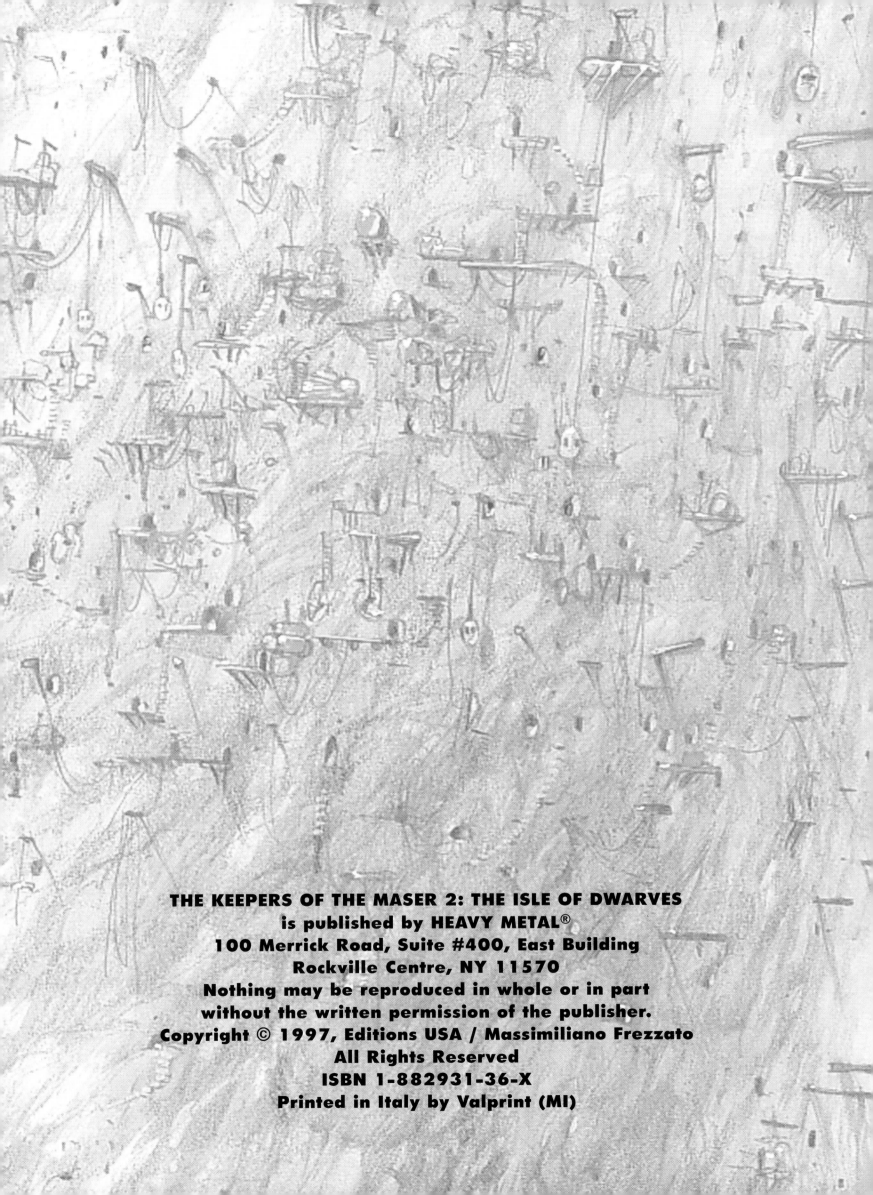

THE KEEPERS OF THE MASER 2: THE ISLE OF DWARVES
is published by HEAVY METAL®
100 Merrick Road, Suite #400, East Building
Rockville Centre, NY 11570
Nothing may be reproduced in whole or in part
without the written permission of the publisher.
Copyright © 1997, Editions USA / Massimiliano Frezzato
All Rights Reserved
ISBN 1-882931-36-X
Printed in Italy by Valprint (MI)

FOR TANIA...

...AND MY SINCERE THANKS TO ADRIANO VELICOGNIA,
TESHI, ROSALIE, FERSHID & THE THOUSANDS OF
FLIES THAT WERE MISTREATED DURING THE
PRODUCTION OF THIS BOOK.

THE COVER ILLUSTRATION FOR 'KOLONY'
AND THE TECHNICAL DRAWINGS OF THE SEWER-RAT,
THE YOK, THE RUST-BUG, THE SNAKE-WORM
AND THE LICHENS WERE RENDERED BY
CINZIA DIFELICE.

KOLONY

THE ESSENTIAL SURVIVAL GUIDE
To make your sojourn on the Lost Planet tolerable
(pleasurable being completely out of the question).

ZERIT

Electric Fingernail:

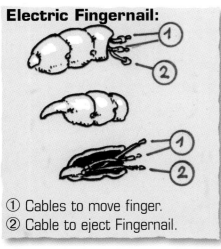

① Cables to move finger.
② Cable to eject Fingernail.

N.B. The battery works on solar energy. When The Tobo is lost in the fog the energy is depleted, making it difficult to eject The Fingernail (p.8, Book 2).

Rockhett:

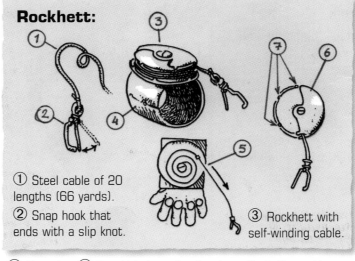

① Steel cable of 20 lengths (66 yards).
② Snap hook that ends with a slip knot.
③ Rockhett with self-winding cable.

④ Bracelet. ⑤ Steel-blade spring for the self-winding cable (its tension adjusts automatically according to the user's weight). ⑥ Torque regulator for cable wind-back. ⑦ Lugs for cable winder (p.12, Book 2).

① Glass shield that flips open, accessing the plug to synchronize the watch with The Tower's terminal. ② Diode to display hours (Hoz). ③ Diode showing minutes (Moz). ④ Plug from The Tower's terminal for instantaneous synchronization (Zerit cannot override this effect, which explains why he's late).

Maser Watch:

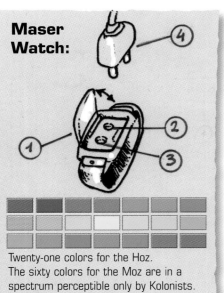

Twenty-one colors for the Hoz.
The sixty colors for the Moz are in a spectrum perceptible only by Kolonists.

- Erha's presumed father.
- Sixty Eiz old.
- Successor to Tusar. He is the new Chief Keeper of The Maser village. His principal role is to receive Maser transmissions. Like all the other Keepers, he uses The drug Clim. He has a mechanical implant in his little finger and is unequalled in his use of The Rockhett.

Zerit's Rockhett has been adjusted to carry only his own weight.

❶ Reader Robot. ❷ Sleeping bag. ❸ Eye patch.
❹ Pilot's helmet made of Yok leather. ❺ Box of Clim.
❻ Rifle. ❼ Aiming device. ❽ Water flask with purifier (spores absorb the salt from sea water).
❾ Yok fat (fuel for the lantern). ❿ Rockhett.
⓫ Maser symbol. ⓬ Maser watch. ⓭ Plates of armor. ⓮ Electric Fingernail. ⓯ Bait for Rust-bugs.

Water flask: with purifier (the spores feed on the salt of the sea wate and make it drinkabl

Massimiliano Frezzato 1994

FANGO

1. Maser Watch.
2. Trinoculars (p.14, Book1).
3. Eye patch.
4. Breastplate.
5. Photos of his family.
6. Set of Keys (mechanical).
7. Water flask with purifier.
8. Ammonia container.
9. Memory banks for Reader Robot (C.I.R.O.).
10. Projectiles.
11. Yok fat.
12. Tool kit.
13. Handgun.

- His name means Mud (according to an old Kolonial legend, all life is created from earth).
- A highly skilled Mechanic, thanks to the presence of his Reader Robot.
- Can read and write.
- Thirty Eiz old.
- Blind in one eye as a result of genetic experiments conducted in ancient Times.
- His parents were scientists who lived in a research outpost detached from The Tower.

TRINOCULARS: tri-optical selective vision.

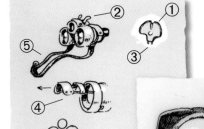

Focal lengths:
A = 7 Ø.
B = 5 Ø.
C = 10 Ø.

① Memory disk (capacity 2 Hoz).
② Vision stabilizers.
③ Auxiliary socket for image projection (p. 18, Book 1).
④ Zoom (anti-reflective with selective vision).
⑤ Shoulder strap.

N.B. The three lenses are independent of one another and may be individually adjusted.

ERHA

- Presumed daughter of Zerit.
- Twenty-seven Eiz old.
- The best pilot in The Maser village.
- A biologist whose ambition is to catalog all the algae and lichens on Kolony.
- As a consequence of the genetic experiments, two fingers of her left hand are gangrened; she suffers from bulimia and from gastric hyper-acidity.
- She has discovered how to distill alcohol (holy water) from fermented lichens.
- Danheel is her daughter. The father's identity remains a mystery.

Erha is a killer with a slingshot.

THE SACRED SYMBOL:
Contains complete maps of The Mother Tower.

① Indication of the floor in relation to the projection.
② Map of the projection of the selected floor.
③ The heart of the Sacred Symbol: the only part that may be touched. The ring around it pushes the fingers away. All the symbols float in the air (p.22, Book 1). Meaning of the Maser Symbol.
④ Socket to The Tower's terminal with automatic location of the floors.

❶ On-board Computer Robot (see Reader Robot). She calls it Robotino. ❷ Sleeping bag. ❸ Her favorite weapon, the slingshot (projectiles: gas grenades). ❹ Eye patch. ❺ Navigation cable. ❻ Sun shades. ❼ Snow goggles. ❽ Lever to remove helmet. ❾ Bazooka. ❿ Earmuffs. ⓫ Box of Clim. ⓬ Ammonia container ⓭ Ammonia dispenser. ⓮ Lighter. ⓯ Yok fat. ⓰ Gun cleaner. ⓱ Monocular. ⓲ Rockhett. ⓳ Maser watch. ⓴ Special glove to retard gangrene proliferation. ㉑ Electric Fingernail. ㉒ Water flask with purifier. ㉓ Holy water. ㉔ Cutlass.

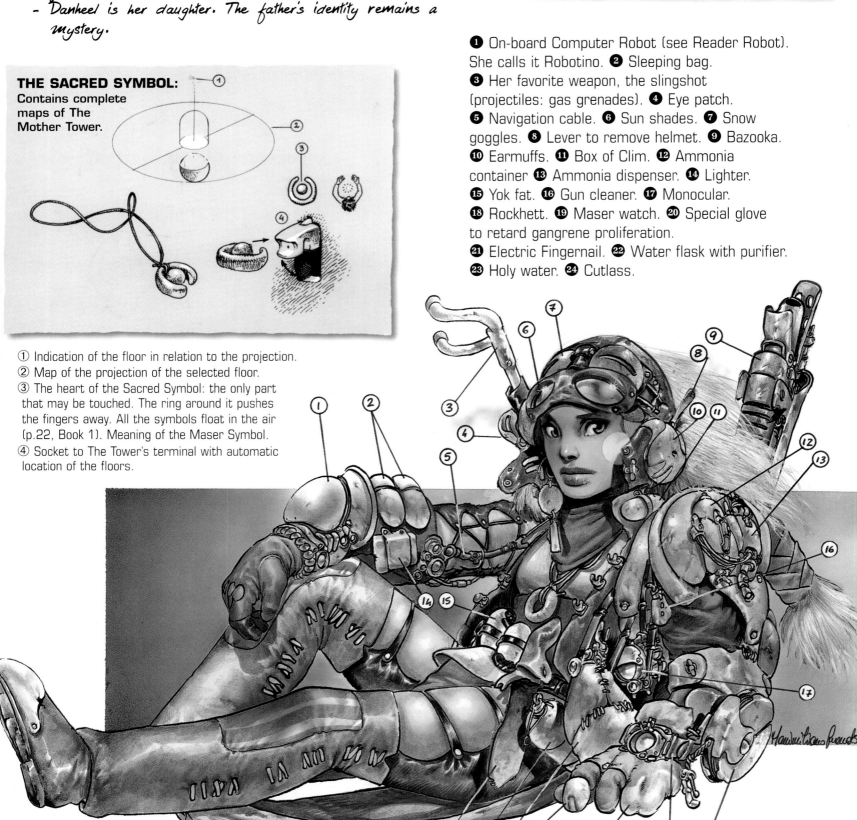

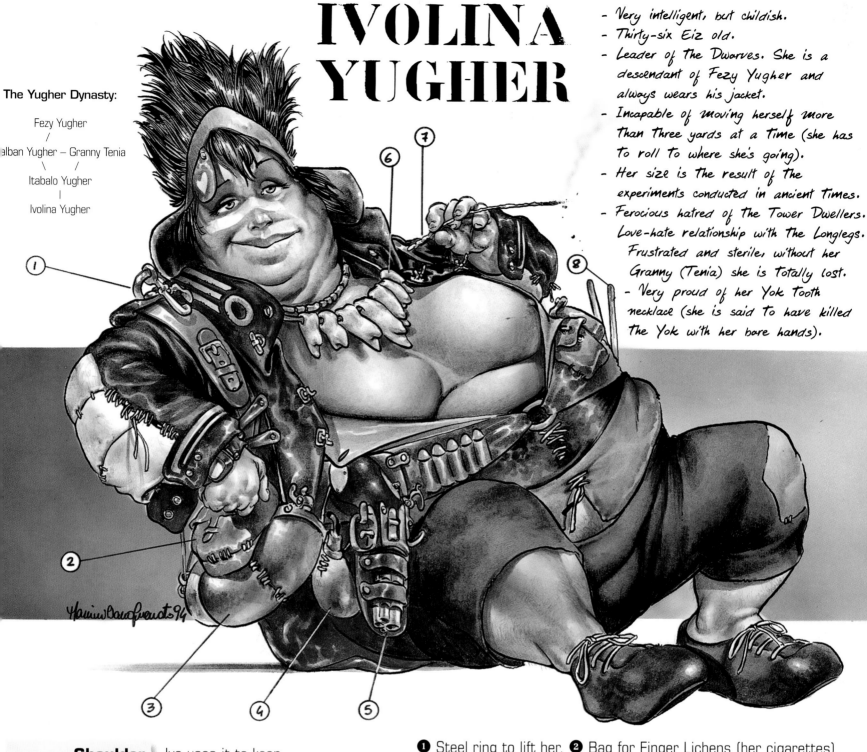

IVOLINA YUGHER

- Very intelligent, but childish.
- Thirty-six Eiz old.
- Leader of The Dwarves. She is a descendant of Fezy Yugher and always wears his jacket.
- Incapable of moving herself more than three yards at a time (she has to roll to where she's going).
- Her size is the result of the experiments conducted in ancient times.
- Ferocious hatred of the Tower Dwellers. Love-hate relationship with The Longlegs. Frustrated and sterile, without her Granny (Tenia) she is totally lost.
- Very proud of her Yok Tooth necklace (she is said to have killed the Yok with her bare hands).

❶ Steel ring to lift her. ❷ Bag for Finger Lichens (her cigarettes). ❸ Water and purifier. ❹ Yok fat. ❺ Handgun. ❻ Necklace. ❼ Cigarette (Finger Lichen). ❽ Back scratcher.

Shoulder Telephone:

Ivo uses it to keep in contact with the Dwarves (p.40, Book 2). It has an incandescent antenna, which is also used to light her Finger Lichen cigarettes. The batteries are powered by Heat-cubes.

Constriction spheres/ handcuffs:

Conceived for and used only on the Dwarves. They prevent the bearer from using his hands. They can be attached together or used individually (p.27, Book 2).

This is how Ivo was carried from the Mother Tower to her Turret (where the Dwarves were holding Zerit prisoner).

THE DWARVES

Funnel to pour in The Gunpowder.

- They were genetically created for hard labor.
- Strong considering Their size, highly resistant and require little sleep.
- Legend has it that They were used To construct The Tower.
- Consume large quantities of Clim (which increases Their capacity To work).
- Low intelligence, very aggressive, kill one another over Trivialities.
- Their community is divided into five social catagories:
1. Ivo's Bodyguards.
2. Engineers and Mechanics.
3. Scouts and Pilots for The Dragonflies.
4. Fishermen and Lichen Gatherers.
5. Women and Children.
- They have blue Tongues (from heavy use of Clim).
- They live in caverns carved into The facade of The Mother Tower.
- Legal Tender: Iron, found in The corridors of The Mother Tower.
- Originally, The eye surgery was meant To improve vision in The dark mines (only The pupil was left exposed). With Time, The operation became a mandatory sacred ritual. A lifetime of pain probably explains Their bad Temper.

Eye surgery (sacred ritual):
① The operation is performed at the age of 2 Eiz.
② Sand is poured under the eyelids which are then sewn together, leaving only the pupil exposed.
③ At the end of 2 Syntribens the stitches are removed. Scarring: 1 Eiz.

DUMB DUMB

Figure(A):
① Large nostril. ② Small nostril. ③ Eyes. ④ Glands that secrete a foam when it is excited. ⑤ Anti-dust plugs for the large nostrils.

Figure(B):
① Climbing hooks made of Yok bone.

Figure(C):
The Dumb Dumb communicates with the aid of a whistle and two flags.

❶ Back covered with a piece of leather (protection from the heavy loads it carries).
❷ The 'Treasure'.
❸ Yok-bone whistle.
❹ Climbing hooks.
❺ Wee-wee.
❻ Dumb Dumb's mother (dead, hence stuffed).

- They are peaceful giant dwarves of incredible strength, but possess The brains of a small bird.
- They are almost incapable of speech and suffer from urinary incontinence.
- They are The only dwarves That underwent further genetic experimentation. Of The Three Dumb Dumbs That were engendered, Two died. This is The only survivor. Of neutral sex, it is sterile (p.24, Book 1).
- It accumulates a 'Treasure' in The pouches of its belt, made up of anything it finds along The way.
- When it is born, its mother dies.

THE ROBOTS

C.I.R.O. & ROBOTINO

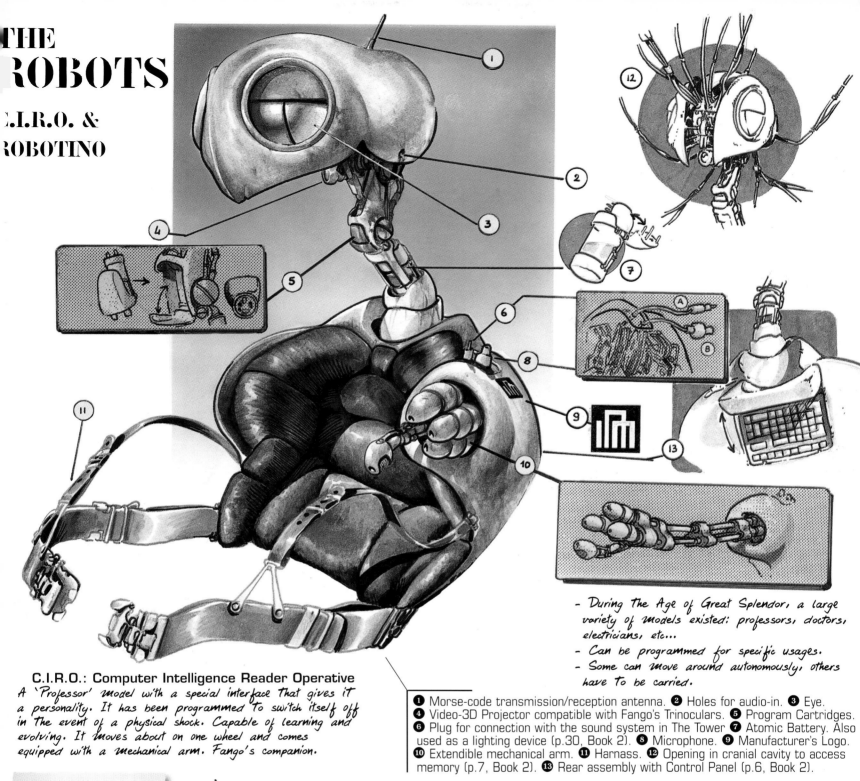

C.I.R.O.: Computer Intelligence Reader Operative

A 'Professor' model with a special interface that gives it a personality. It has been programmed to switch itself off in the event of a physical shock. Capable of learning and evolving. It moves about on one wheel and comes equipped with a mechanical arm. Fango's companion.

- During The Age of Great Splendor, a large variety of models existed: professors, doctors, electricians, etc....
- Can be programmed for specific usages.
- Some can move around autonomously, others have to be carried.

❶ Morse-code transmission/reception antenna. ❷ Holes for audio-in. ❸ Eye. ❹ Video-3D Projector compatible with Fango's Trinoculars. ❺ Program Cartridges. ❻ Plug for connection with the sound system in The Tower ❼ Atomic Battery. Also used as a lighting device (p.30, Book 2). ❽ Microphone. ❾ Manufacturer's Logo. ❿ Extendible mechanical arm. ⓫ Harnass. ⓬ Opening in cranial cavity to access memory (p.7, Book 2). ⓭ Rear assembly with Control Panel (p.6, Book 2).

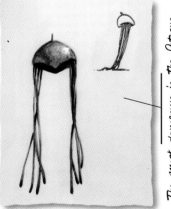

- The most dangerous is The Octopus model, but those who have seen one are no longer around to talk about it...

Robotino:

① Command Keyboard. ② & ⑤ Wheel allowing the Robot to move across a map. ③ Microcamera for aerial reconnaissance. ④ Map-reading lens. ⑥ Pencil Finger. Also used to connect itself to the main computer (p.2, Book 2). ⑦ Cutting Finger. ⑧ Compass Finger. ⑨ Goniometric Finger. ⑩ Finger for measuring distances.

Robotino aka The Saint Bernard Robot:
- *When reading Traditional maps, it can establish precise distances, navigation routes, exact positions, coordinates, etc....*
- *Almost indispensable in piloting an 'Owl' (see planes) to the maximum of its capacities.*
- *It does not have speech capabilities.*

There are many other models of Reader Robots, such as the mysterious T.M.N.T. (p.6, Book 2).

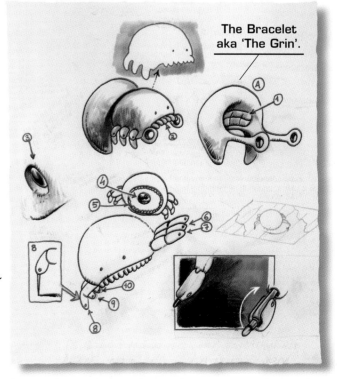

The Bracelet aka 'The Grin'.

PLANES: THE OWL

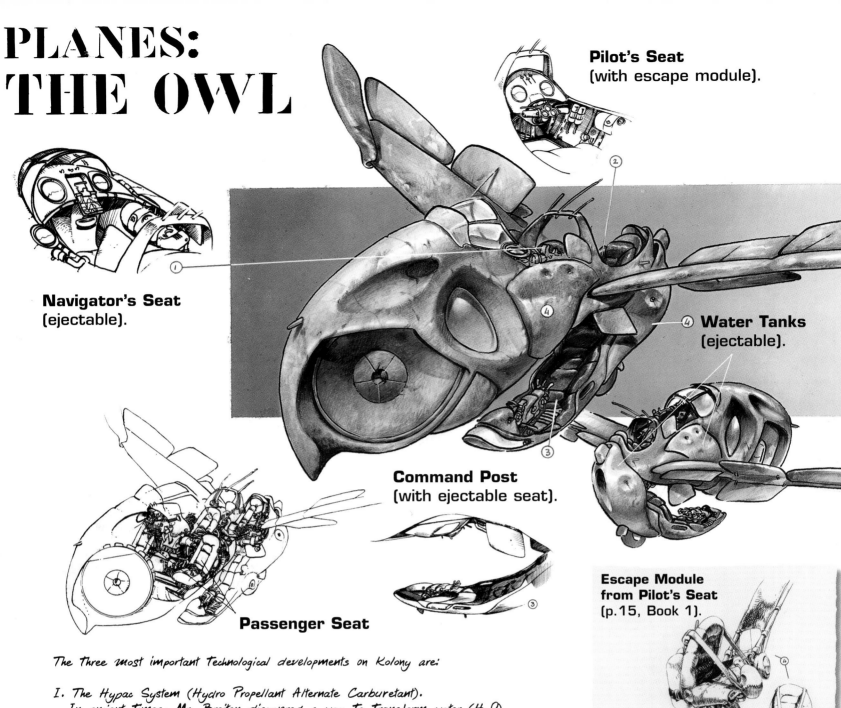

Pilot's Seat
(with escape module).

Navigator's Seat
(ejectable).

④ **Water Tanks**
(ejectable).

Command Post
(with ejectable seat).

Passenger Seat

**Escape Module
from Pilot's Seat**
(p.15, Book 1).

The Three most important Technological developments on Kolony are:

I. The Hypac System (Hydro Propellant Alternate Carburetant).
In ancient Times, Mr. Breiten discovered a way To Transform water (H_2O)
into a combustible fuel by The fission of Two molecules of Hydrogen and one
of Oxygen using The Heat-cubes (p.36, Book 1). The Hydrogen act3 as
fuel, while The Oxygen is eliminated with The impurities in The water, such as
sea salt and other organic residues. The slag That is left in The Tanks of The
planes is Then cleaned out with Ammonia.

II. The Micro-Wing System:
The planes are controlled by an on-board computer (atmospheric-friction
sensometer) and have a system of Micro Wings To compensate for air friction.
The Micro Wings are constantly in motion insuring The plane's fluid Trajectory.

III. Hyper Steel:
It has exactly The same characteristics as Steel, but is Twenty Times lighter.
All The planes on Kolony are made of This metal.

* **Micro Wings.**

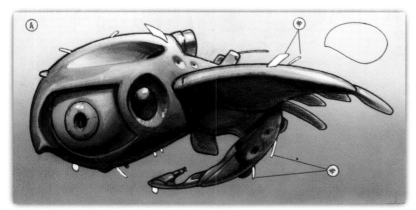

Figure A – Cargo Plane (Zerit).

Figure B – Fighter Plane (Erha).

THE DRAGONFLY

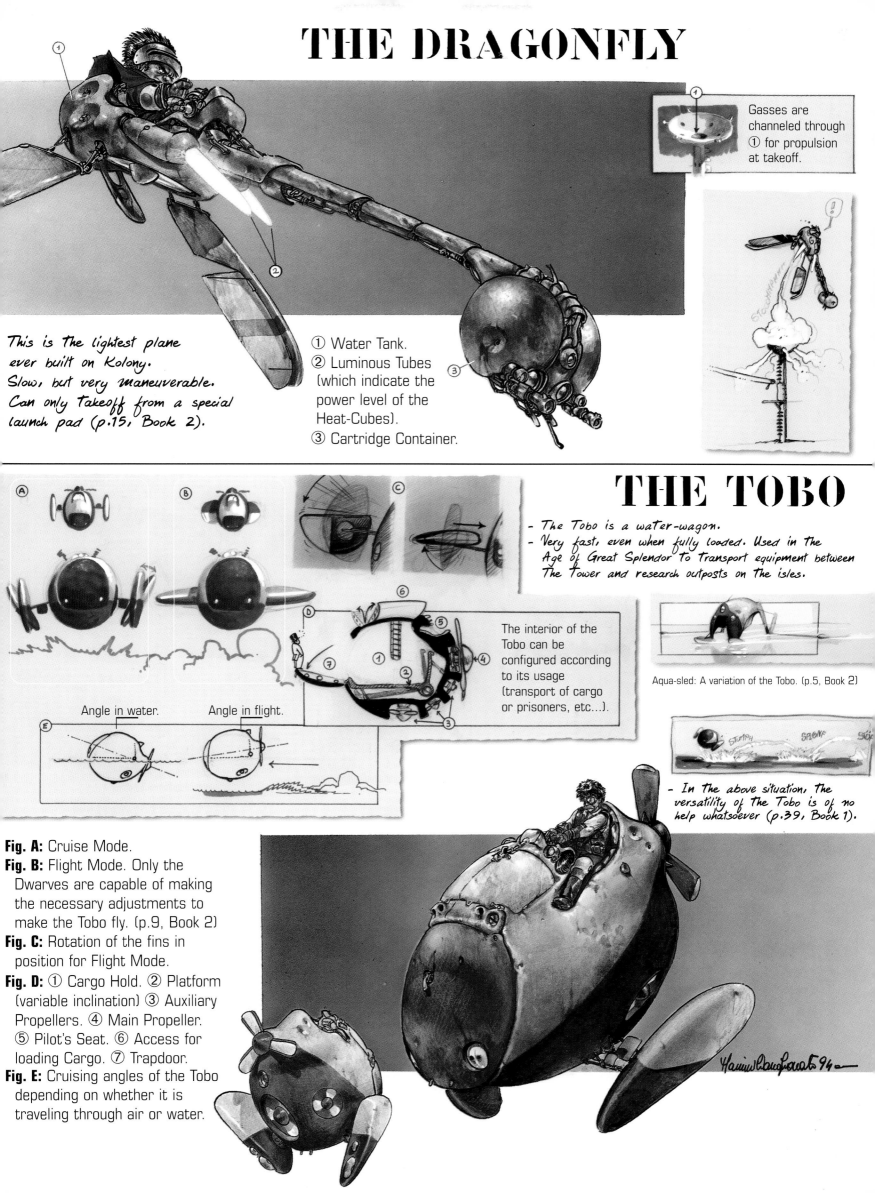

Gasses are channeled through ① for propulsion at takeoff.

This is the lightest plane ever built on Kolony. Slow, but very maneuverable. Can only takeoff from a special launch pad (p.15, Book 2).

① Water Tank.
② Luminous Tubes (which indicate the power level of the Heat-Cubes).
③ Cartridge Container.

THE TOBO

- The Tobo is a water-wagon.
- Very fast, even when fully loaded. Used in the Age of Great Splendor to transport equipment between the Tower and research outposts on the isles.

The interior of the Tobo can be configured according to its usage (transport of cargo or prisoners, etc...).

Aqua-sled: A variation of the Tobo. (p.5, Book 2)

- In the above situation, the versatility of the Tobo is of no help whatsoever (p.39, Book 1).

Angle in water.   Angle in flight.

Fig. A: Cruise Mode.
Fig. B: Flight Mode. Only the Dwarves are capable of making the necessary adjustments to make the Tobo fly. (p.9, Book 2)
Fig. C: Rotation of the fins in position for Flight Mode.
Fig. D: ① Cargo Hold. ② Platform (variable inclination) ③ Auxiliary Propellers. ④ Main Propeller. ⑤ Pilot's Seat. ⑥ Access for loading Cargo. ⑦ Trapdoor.
Fig. E: Cruising angles of the Tobo depending on whether it is traveling through air or water.

SEWER RAT

Muridæ Auratus

- The Sewer Rat is the result of genetic experiments.
- Much sought after for its delicate meat, its fine fur, but mainly because it produces Clim, The most popular drug on Kolony (p.23, Book 1).
- It has Two pairs of ultra-sensitive ears.

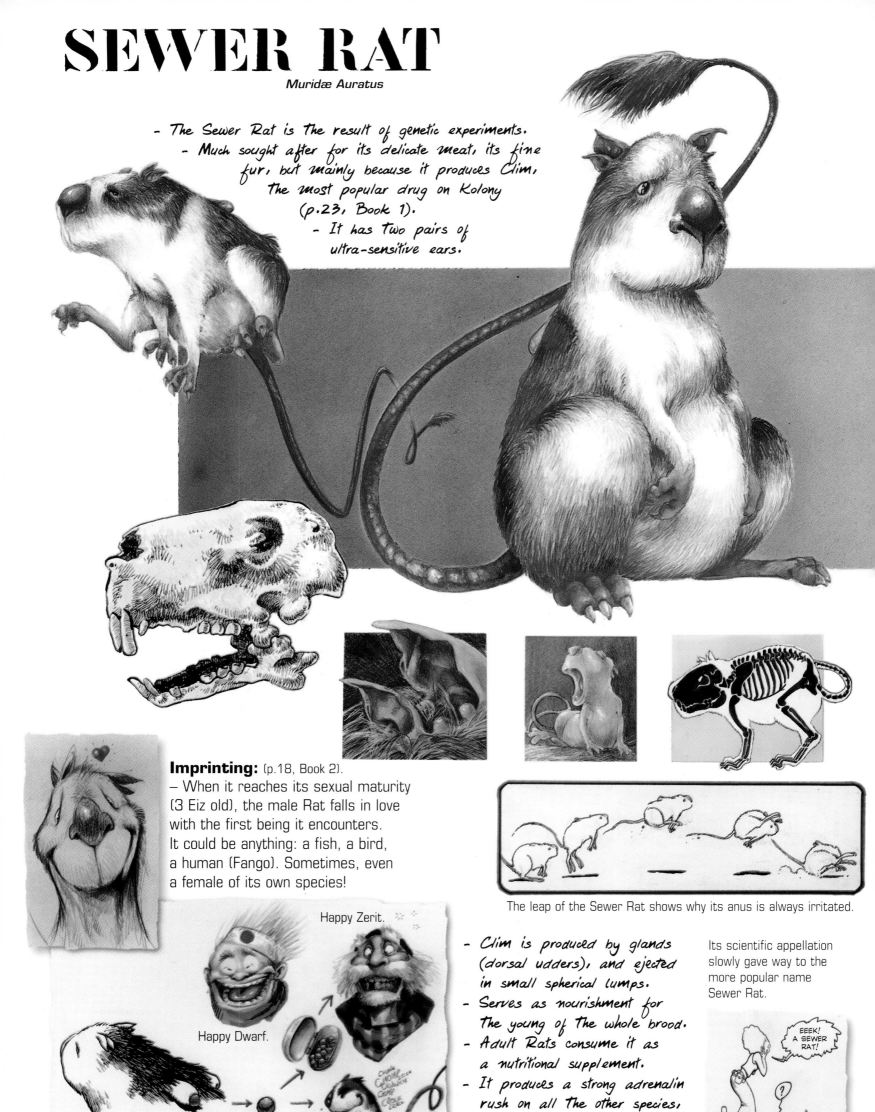

Imprinting: (p.18, Book 2).
– When it reaches its sexual maturity (3 Eiz old), the male Rat falls in love with the first being it encounters. It could be anything: a fish, a bird, a human (Fango). Sometimes, even a female of its own species!

The leap of the Sewer Rat shows why its anus is always irritated.

Happy Zerit.

Happy Dwarf.

Happy Rat.

- Clim is produced by glands (dorsal udders), and ejected in small spherical lumps.
- Serves as nourishment for The young of The whole brood.
- Adult Rats consume it as a nutritional supplement.
- It produces a strong adrenalin rush on all The other species, who regard it as a powerful energizing drug.

Its scientific appellation slowly gave way to the more popular name Sewer Rat.

EEEK! A SEWER RAT!

?

YOK

Serrasalamus Cetacea

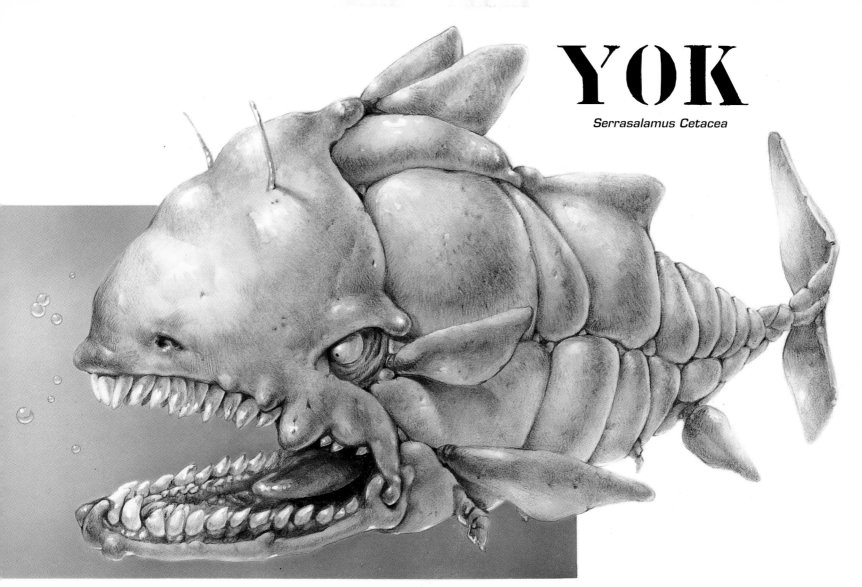

- A gigantic amphibian creature.
- Cemeteries full of skeletons have been found (p.25, Book 2).
- Out of the water, it moves about with the help of its small ventricular fins.
- An Omnivorous creature.
- The Yok is the most mysterious animal on Kolony.
- At birth, the baby Yok has four eyes that slowly merge into one pair as it gets older.
- Its exterior 'plates' are used as armor by the Kolonists.

- Few have lived to boast of having been toe to toe with a Yok; Fango is one of them (p.31, Book 1).

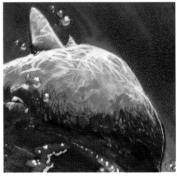

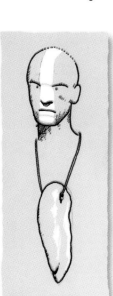

Yok teeth are considered very precious and are often displayed as trophies or worn as jewelry (Cf. : Ivo p.27, T.2).

No one has ever seen a baby Yok. The illustration below, is an artist's impression.

Recently, Yoks have been committing mass suicide for no apparent reason.

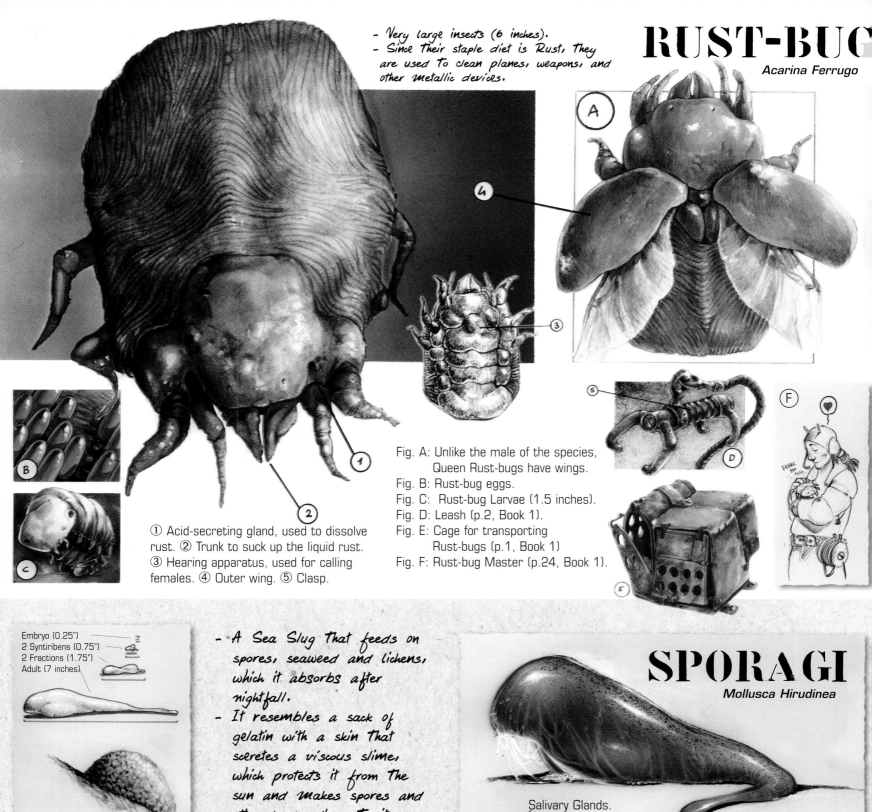

RUST-BUG
Acarina Ferrugo

- Very large insects (6 inches).
- Since their staple diet is Rust, they are used to clean planes, weapons, and other metallic devices.

Fig. A: Unlike the male of the species, Queen Rust-bugs have wings.
Fig. B: Rust-bug eggs.
Fig. C: Rust-bug Larvae (1.5 inches).
Fig. D: Leash (p.2, Book 1).
Fig. E: Cage for transporting Rust-bugs (p.1, Book 1)
Fig. F: Rust-bug Master (p.24, Book 1).

① Acid-secreting gland, used to dissolve rust. ② Trunk to suck up the liquid rust. ③ Hearing apparatus, used for calling females. ④ Outer wing. ⑤ Clasp.

SPORAGI
Mollusca Hirudinea

- A Sea Slug that feeds on spores, seaweed and lichens, which it absorbs after nightfall.
- It resembles a sack of gelatin with a skin that secretes a viscous slime, which protects it from the sun and makes spores and other food adhere to it.
- The favorite food of the Yoks.

Embryo (0.25")
2 Syntiribens (0.75")
2 Fractions (1.75")
Adult (7 inches)

Salivary Glands.

- The Sporagi reproduce themselves through parthenogenesis.
- They attach themselves to a rock and develop larvae under their skin, which takes on the consistency of stone. This form is known as 'bulbous rock' and is very difficult to distinguish from a large pebble.

① Gas Mask: The Dwarves use live Sporagi to filter toxic gasses out of the air. Inconvenience: The Sporagi continue secreting slime inside the mask. ② Their viscosity makes them almost impossible to cut open. ③ Sporagi Trap. ④ Cauldron used for cooking the Sporagi. The broth is considered very nutritious.

③ **Sporagi Trap:**

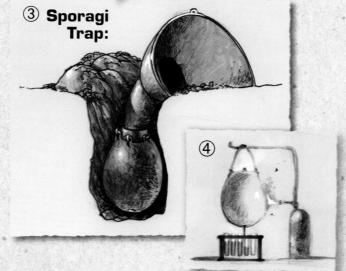

① **Gas Mask:**

②

SNAKE-WORM
Viperidæ Acanthocephala

- Its flesh is the favorite food of the Survivors.
- Every part of its body is used (Tools, weapons, jewelry...).

Fig. A: Tracks left by Snake-worms.

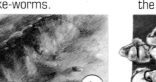

Fig. B: Jewelry made from the rings of Snake-worms.

① Head. ② Carapace.
③ Anus.

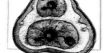

Cross section of a Snake-worm.

- Folded in two under its carapace, the Snake-worm is in fact twice as long as it appears to be.
- Hunting Snake-worms can be very dangerous as they may unexpectedly break surface and strike a leg to deposit their larvae (see Fig. D).

Hunting Snake-worms:
Fig. A: ① Finding the Spoor. ② Hooking. ③ Running. ④ The capture.

Fig. C: Hook for hunting Snake-worms.

SPIDER-FLY
Araneæ Muscaria

- The larva of the Spider-fly leaves a slimy trail behind it which attracts its prey to the brood (Fig. B).

Fig. A: Eggs.
Fig. B: Larva.
Fig. C: Adult.

The Queen:

Her wings flap incessantly to cool the royal chamber.

Her web protects the eggs.

The gas used by the Dwarves as a disinfectant is extracted from the web of the Spider-fly; it has a narcotic effect.

① Area for the Swarm.
② Larvae (come out only to feed).
③ The Royal Chamber.
④ Incubation area for the eggs.

- When a foot touches the ground, the vibrations of the web indicate the weight and the position of the future victim.
- The web has narcotic properties, which make the victim lose consciousness and then slowly dissolve.

- If you see this hovering in front of your face, you may be sure that there are millions of its kind close behind and that thy end is nigh.

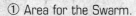

The Attack:
Direction of wind

- A thick mesh of webs covers the ground protecting the Spider-flies from the cold.

- The number of Spider-flies that attack is directly proportional to the victim's weight.

ISLE OF DWARVES

Ivolina Yugher's Turret:

❶ Pivoting roof. ❷ Hangar for the 'Owl'. ❸ Section of solid iron for counterweight. ❹ Hangar for the 'Dragonflies'. ❺ Mobile Platform for takeoff. ❻ Area where the Turret's Cannon was housed. Now, Ivo's Room (p.27, Book 2). ❼ Air shafts through which Fango and Erha fell (p.40, Book 2). ❽ Area from which the Cannon used to be loaded. Now, Dwarves' meeting room (p.42, Book 2).

❾ Recoil pad for the Cannon. Now, the mobile floor of Ivo's Room (p.39, Book 2). ❿ Projectiles for the Cannon. Now, filled with hundreds of enraged Dwarves. ⓫ & ⓬ Former living quarters of the Tower Dwellers. Now, empty. ⓭ Hangar for the Tobos. This is where the Dumb Dumb enters when he brings Fango to Ivo (p.37, Book 2). ⓮ Exit for the Tobos. Now, the entrance to the Turret. ⓯ Lateral Wall. ⓰ Corridor for inspection and maintenance of the wall. ⓱ Mechanism that makes the Turret rotate. ⓲ Engine for the Turret. ⓳ The Rampart promenade.

Ivo's Room: (p.27, Book 2).

Fig. A:

① Roof of the Tower where Zerit and Fango land with the Tobo (p.11, Book .2).
② Granny Tenia's Terrace, where Fango falls through the floor (p.23, Book 2).
③ This is where Fango ends his fall (p.30, Book 2).
④ Dwarf Cave (p.12, Book 2).
⑤ Canals (p.17, Book 2).
⑥ Ivo's Turret (p.17, Book 2).

Fig. B:

The Isle is surrounded by a ring of fog made up of volcanic vapor, making it impossible to navigate (p.42, Book 1).

Detail of the outside wall of the Mother Tower.

Cross section of the Mother Tower:

◉ The Dumb Dumb's route, with Fango on his back (p.31, 37, Book 2).

◉ Submerged Areas.

- The Dam: There are about forty dams on The Isle of Dwarves which are used to regulate the water level of the canals (p. 17, Book 2).

GEOGRAPHY

The habitable zone on Kolony:

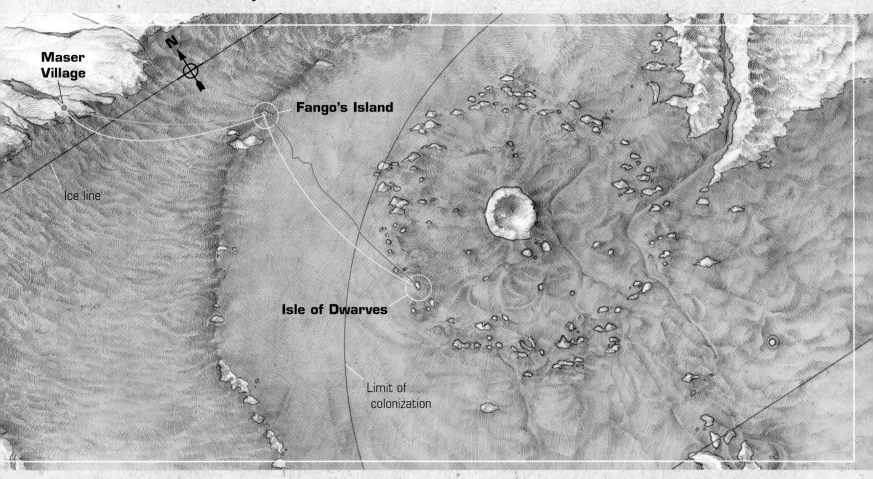

Maser Village

N

Ice line

Fango's Island

Isle of Dwarves

Limit of
colonization

▭ : Zerit's Route.   ▭ : Erha's Route.   ▬ : Zerit & Fango's Route.

DETAILS

Letters:

(Example p.14, Book 1. Look out for others...).

Figures:

$$\boxed{26} = \begin{matrix} E & H \\ I & I \\ R & A \end{matrix} = ERHA$$

The Alphabet:
- The symbols correspond to the 26 letters of our alphabet.
- In writing, the letters are paired off in twos. (Example p.14, Book 1. Look out for others...).

The Lichens: ① Cabbage Lichen: edible. ② Cotton Lichen: used as stuffing. ③ Finger Lichen: used as cigarettes by Ivo and to distill Erha's 'holy water'. ④ Idiot's Lichen: only an idiot can't differentiate this from a Cabbage Lichen. ⑤ Musk Lichen: edible. ⑥ Red-death Lichen: inedible, highly poisonous.

The Experiments:

- Legend has it that in ancient times biogenetic experiments were conducted. The questions Where? Why? How? and By whom? remain unanswered to this day. But the whole population of Kolony seems to have been affected in some way (p.20, T.2).

The Survivors:

- They are scattered all over Kolony wherever climate permits living conditions.
- No one knows how many actually exist or where they are. Fango is one of them but he doesn't know it (p.32, Book 2).
- Each individual, or group of Survivors, is unaware of the existence of the others.

The Tatoos:

On reaching the age of reason each individual is tatooed with a symbol indicating his character and his potential. Far example, the tatoo on Fango's chin indicates a slight feeblemindedness. The Dumb Dumb's tatoo is much more imposing. In the case of a complete idiot, the tatoo goes all the way up his forehead.

Erha is an authority on the study and classification of lichens. Throughout her extensive research she has been able to establish that there is no proof whatsoever of the existence of a Masked Cucumber on the explored surface of Kolony.

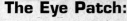

The Eye Patch: Eye patches were originally conceived for the Dwarves to protect their eyes during the construction of The Tower, the sunlight being particularly blinding on the exposed exterior (Fig.A). It has since become a tradition to wear them and those who don't are looked down upon.